Gray Rabbit's Odd One Out

Alan Baker

KINGFISHER

NEW YORK

KINGFISHER
LONDON & NEW YORK

Copyright © Alan Baker 1995

Published in the United States by Kingfisher,
175 Fifth Avenue, New York, NY 10010
Kingfisher is an imprint of Macmillan Children's Books, London.
All rights reserved.

Distributed in the U.S. by Macmillan,
175 Fifth Avenue, New York, NY 10010
Distributed in Canada by H.B. Fenn and Company Ltd.,
34 Nixon Road, Bolton, Ontario L7E 1W2

LIBRARY OF CONGRESS CATALOGING-IN-PUBLICATION DATA
Baker, Alan.
Gray Rabbit's Odd One Out/Alan Baker.
—1st American ed.
p.   cm. — (Little rabbit books)
Summary: Gray Rabbit tidies up his room and sorts his belongings
into groups of his favorite things as he searches for his favorite book.
[1. Orderliness—Fiction. 2. Rabbits—Fiction.]
I. Title. II. Series: Baker, Alan. Little rabbit books.
PZ7.B1688Bn 1995
[E]—dc20 94-42002 CIP AC

ISBN 978-0-7534-5257-8

Printed in Singapore

6 8 10 9 7

For more information, please visit
www.kingfisherpublications.com

One morning Gray Rabbit could
not find his favorite book.

It's time to clean up, thought Rabbit.
First let's sort out the wooden animals.

There were two of each kind—just like in Noah's ark.

But one thing was not an animal.
What was the odd one out?

A teaspoon.

So Rabbit sorted out his cups and saucers.
But one thing did not belong.
What was it?

A paintbrush.

Rabbit gathered up his paints and brushes and made a useful sign. Now what was the odd one out?

A red and yellow polka-dot ball.

Rabbit found all his round things.
Hey, stop rolling away!
But one thing did not belong.
What was it?

A purple vase.
Where can that go? thought Rabbit.
It's the only vase I have.

Then he matched it up with all the other purple things. But something wasn't purple. What was it?

A duck. That belonged with the other stuffed animals, so Rabbit lined them all up in a row.

Now what did not belong?

A block.

There were lots and lots of blocks.
How could Rabbit sort them out?

First he built a square
of red blocks,

then a wall
of green blocks.

The yellow blocks made a tower.
What was that among the blue blocks?

Look! Rabbit's favorite book.
I'll sort out the blue blocks,
he thought, then I'll read
my story.

At last!